TRAVEL

an anthology of microlit

edited by

Cassandra Atherton

SPINELESS WONDERS
www.shortaustralianstories.com.au

A catalogue record for this book is available from the National Library of Australia

Travel, trouble, music, art, a kiss, a frock, a rhyme --
I never said they feed my heart, but still they pass my time.
DOROTHY PARKER

Contents

THE JOANNE BURNS AWARD

ABOUT JOANNE BURNS

Introduction

In the current Covid world, it seems apt that TRAVEL should be the theme for an anthology of micro literature. The wide world seems suddenly diminished as many people who are used to going abroad find themselves staying still. At the same time, this is when the imagination can carry us great distances. The works in this anthology show that there is no locking down the human imagination, and even as we stay put physically, part of us can still depart.

With microlit, a reader can traverse many diverse places in a short span of time and with very few words – moods and settings can change in an instant. Certain pieces in this collection highlight this aspect of the genre. In a moment, we are on the train with Restless Addie, moving through car after moving train car in a way that only microlit allows through its sheer compression.

Indeed, with the pieces curated here by Cassandra Atherton, readers travel elsewhere in a flash. And with this collection, we visit a variety of places in different ways– geographically, metaphorically, emotionally – sometimes all in a single work. For example, we travel through time, age, and memory—all simultaneously—with Sandra Renew's 'The Amazing Sinking Car'.

Works like Stuart A. Barnes's piece offers a metaphoric journey as it takes us on a whirlwind tour through poems about travel – one phrase at time, stopping at some of my favorite lines by William Stafford, e.e. Cummings, and Robert Frost.

In Dominique Hecq's 'Cursive', we gallivant through the curves of fonts and letters, on a journey about inscribing words even as we are reading them. Pieces like this stay with a reader, much like snippets of travel memories will, and appear unbidden. For example, days after reading this collection, as I made a grocery list, 'Cursive' sprang to mind.

Ultimately, through these pieces, we are invited to consider the relative meaning of 'travel' and how 'travel' has changed since the pandemic began. Susan McCreery's piece shows how, on some days, traveling the length of the bed is movement enough. And Jo Tuscano's 'The Hardest Trek I've Ever Done' takes us through a standard day of living in lockdown, demonstrating how sometimes simply surviving is the greatest journey of all.

Suddenly, virtual walls thrown up by a virus that is too small to see with the naked eye has many writers and readers reimagining, pondering how to contend with, acknowledge, and/or subvert these walls. *TRAVEL: an anthology of microlit* serves as an unconventional travel book, transporting readers in unexpected ways before they even realise they have left.

—Kimberly K. Williams, 2022

From The Editor

Congratulations to those shortlisted for the 2022 Newcastle Writers Festival/joanne burns Microlit Award and to all of the writers who entered the competition. The response to this year's theme was unprecedented. We tapped a vein of yearning and creativity which made shortlisting a finite number of pieces really challenging. And whilst the task was daunting, the opportunity to travel vicariously to so many places and times was welcome compensation for our locked-down existence.

Thank you to Rosemarie Milsom, director of the Newcastle Writers Festival and her team for her foresight in sponsoring this award and her phenomenal work in bringing it to the fabu¬lous Newcastle Writers Festival – one of the finest and most supportive writers' festivals in Australia.

Thank you to the commissioned writers from both Australia and the United States of America: Shady Cosgrove, Paul Hetherington, Richard Holt, Holly Iglesias, Peter Johnson, Alyson Miller, Jonathan Penton, Julia Prendergast, Dominic Symes and Paul Venzo. Their wonderfully textured microlit 'travel' pieces certainly showcase the myriad possibilities for the short form. Thank you to Bettina Kaiser for her evocative cover design. Thank you to joanne burns, after whom this award is named and who this year was co-judge. joanne is a pioneer and ambassador of the short form and her luminous, witty and innovative microlit is enduring.

Finally, thank you to Spineless Wonders' publisher, Bronwyn Mehan, for her devotion to the short form and pioneering microlit in Australia. We appreciate her tireless efforts of her team to provide writers with exciting ways to showcase their work both on the page and in the most amazing ways off the page.

—Cassandra Atherton, 2022

Paul Venzo

ZUEL DI QUA, ZUEL DI LÀ

A car, a train, a bus, a plane. Tarmac. A bus, another car. 24 hours leapfrogging one nasal diphthong to another. Pink limestone monoliths. Coffee treacles from gifted hands. A black station-wagon waiting, my features in its gleaming flanks. Barely conscious after hourless sleep, plumped up with sticky pastry, roaring towards Valdobbiadene. Along this road I change into myself. From a duffel bag I produce 'he who craves a cigarette upon waking', 'he who wears linen and sandshoes together'. Disgorged. Served prosecco. Faced with a dozen long-stemmed iterations of dry to very dry to cats-bum-fucking-dry-as-fuck. Tognon – tuba-playing ex-Carabinieri rally driver – mid-vineyard. He is *leggermente* fermented. Backwaters and byways of Zuel di Qua and Zuel di Là. Zanzotto is underfoot, on lips – a salivation. No one's heard of the man. 'A *poet*?' Finally, Milena knew him. A depressed flirt. We toast to that. Tognon in the evening light, black and white, glass in hand, over a deal-wood table. Best photo never posted, but ever taken. A profile, a cameo, for memory's locket.

Holly Iglesias

HITCHED

*It is a work of images, difficult
and bare. Very slow. Like falling in love.*
—Stephanie Strickland, 'Love That Gives Us Ourselves'

They said it was treason to leave the country, though they also said, *Love it or leave it.* America—we loved it by leaving it. Bereft, we left, worked over by the work of images. Burning flag, burning cities, burning girl running through a rice paddy toward the camera, that heap of images left stashed away in closets along with school rings and trinkets and letters bound in ribbon until language itself faded into silence. We learned a new vocabulary from signs on the walls and doors of Zaragoza—carniceria, peligro, policía, ayuntamiento, casa de huéspedes, Carretera de Extremadura. ¡Extremadura!—the word itself a dry, rocky crag of sound and meaning, one of us hearing banishment, defeat, the other mystery and initiation. Which one of us would set foot to the blacktop first and stick out a thumb to catch a ride proved to be the biggest surprise of all.

Catherine Moffat

THE LIGHT REMEMBERED

Perched on the edge of the surf pool he unstraps his leg, puts it aside. Tenderly unwraps his stump. Dives. Swims laps. Up, down. Underwater the world is green and sand, the light a remembered moment. Sunlight is skewed, slanted, tastes of salt. He wears a seaweed wreath, pauses to watch a fish flick from the water. Hauls himself back from the ocean.
On land he sprawls, basking between cement and sun. Slumbers amongst leathered, weathered, walrus men. Cradles his head in the gentle swing of his spring-steel leg.

Peter Johnson

MAIDEN VOYAGE

'The ocean undulating like an experienced lover.' 'Dark, sad clouds wanting to merge and pleasure and themselves.' 'The sunrise craving to slip into something sexy.' All three, dumb expressions repeating themselves in my head like the rat-a-tat-tat of a claw hammer. I'm the last living passenger on this 'maiden' voyage, which, ironically, included only men. The cattle, sick of being sacrificed, had jumped overboard, so the crew was forced to eat each other. The last mariner, mad from guilt and shame, voluntarily walked the plank to the great applause of perched seagulls, while a billionaire in a cowboy hat floated weightlessly in space, too stupid to realize he'd eventually have to land. And me? I'm leaning over the bow, grasping a bouquet of dead roses in my sunburnt hands. I'm waiting for that previously promised maiden to present herself and prove that she is more than just hunger-driven, muzzled memory. I'm praying for a new garden of delights and disappointments to suddenly appear on the horizon. A place where we can happily repopulate, knowing we will be dead long before our watered-down genes ruin it again.

Penelope Layland

GONE, ABSCONDED, ESCAPED, DISAPPEARED

Summoned from slumber by the tinkle of the breakfast trolley somewhere ahead in Business Class, Cynthia immediately saw that the man in the window seat beside her was dead: wide-eyed, empurpled with surprise. Cynthia touched the button to summon the cabin crew.

'I'm a doctor.' Cynthia calmly addressed the attendant's widening eyes. Her boarding pass, doubling as a book mark in her lap, confirmed it. So too, her name, heading Chapter Three, though the attendant could not know that.

'If you could ...' the attendant gestured.

Cynthia unclipped her seatbelt, reached, rested fingertips on the dead man's chill, moist neck.

'Indications of homoeoteleuton,' she murmured, glancing at the attendant. 'Abiit, abscessit, evasit, erupit'—each pronouncement accompanied by interrogative dabs upon the dead man's jaw, lips, temple, lids. There seemed little else to say.

A blanket was efficiently arranged, the seatbelt re-buckled above the swaddle.

Cynthia brushed away the offer of another seat. After all, the plane had begun its descent, and she was only part-way through a rival academic's chapter on Virgil's Georgics. Her own chapter on 'case rhyme' was more prominently placed, she reflected, complacently, reaching for the reading light.

Richard Holt

STILLNESS

Restless Addie does the length of the thundering train. Over and over. Pushes through the gangway doors between the carriages.

Addie's as tall as a basketballer. Lanky and ageing - a difficult combination. Hunch and she might fold like a windblown wheat stalk.

Heading into Winchester, Addie's walking front-to-back just as the old steam locomotive slows to a walking pace. As she pushes through, past a group of sprawling songsters, Addie and the earth are together, the same patch of oil-soaked ground remaining beneath her and only the train moving. Sliding between them both like a magician's cloth.

It's all relative. The earth spins and orbits. The universe expands. Everything moves, all the time, some way. But it's the planet that matters most. How Addie is upon it. And at that moment she is still, perhaps for the longest waking time since she was a girl. She passes all the way through to the card players in the second-last carriage before the connection breaks as the train decelerates, sliding into Winchester to take on coal.

Dominique Hecq

CURSIVE

I hate Times Roman. Love Chancery Cursive. Love chance. Love gallivanting around the word. Chancery Cursive captures how the hand runs across the page. How letters get excited at the beginning of a piece. How they flourish in movement. Cursive lids the light. Echoes mind-chambers and smells of honeysuckle. It gives body to sans-serif. Chancery Cursive takes off like writing in which the letters are joined and formed rapidly without lifting the nib of your pen, from the French *cursif*, from the Medieval Latin *cursivus*, from the Latin *cursus*, all run-running words. Even the past participle *currere*, meaning to run, from the Indo-European root **kers* that always reminds me what a curse a running hand is. Chancery Cursive is a marathon runner. It is tall and lean. It lives vertically, though it does embrace the wind in its course. It thrives on air, blood and water, seeds and nuts. Breeds dream-begotten strokes, forms, letters. *See how they run* away from Times Roman.

PS Cottier

NOT SO GNOMIC

why drag us into air, when we love earth, prefer the dank cave, the spade in hand and the plenitude of worm? we don't care for the jolly photos you send home with our peaked caps touching Mont Blanc, or carefully replicating the metal prong of that famous French tower. we would return to our own small plot, stay stolid and quiet, awakening at night to feast on slumbering fairies and quaint snails, to train toads and smoke pipes packed with pungent toadstool. no, we don't want to sway in New Orleans. Ubud holds no charm for our concrete feet and minds.

Helen Hopcroft

VERSAILLES

We wait. Birds swoop and swing past, pausing to crap on the head of a heroic statue of Louis XIV. Louis' bronze stallion flicks its tail coquettishly, ungelded and elaborately ribboned, easily upstaging his royal master. Fat grey pigeons cluster along window tops, the unexpected swoop of a pointed-winged seagull, large crows bitterly voice their eternal complaints, the occasional tern flicks past. I fiddle with a piece of paper in my jean pocket, hoping that my forty-eight hour museum pass still works. The line creeps forward in a slow shuffle. Nine steps, eleven, eventually the excitement of twenty-seven. Children chatter excitedly. Adults pull food out of paper bags, snack while scanning their phones: neither activity seems to bring much pleasure. The pattern of slow steps recurs: three, nine, eleven. Overhead, an immense blue sky. Five, six, seven. The gates are much closer now. Finally, a magnificent golden fence, decorated with scallop shells and crown motifs at the top, looms up from the densely packed cobblestones. A perfect symbol of wealth and class, the gilded barrier that still divides our world. When the line pushes up against the fence, I notice that gold paint is flaking off in places.

Jonathan Penton

FLEEING HURRICANE IDA

Thirty-six hours to landfall. The rural roads are empty, but Kapoor-black; highways with a posted speed of 70mph turn sharply without warning. Each time I brake you startle awake. The gas stations, empty of fuel, are closed, and we both have to pee.

The cat cries, steadily, for four hours. The radio cuts out and around to various saccharine stations. The rural drivers, more accustomed to these low ways, zip past us with unnerving buzz.

But this is not our first time on this trek. It will not be the last time we run away. We'll stay and run and stay until there's nothing to run from.

Moya Costello

MATILDA

Tilda found herself unexpectedly and inconsolably nomadic. She had thought of herself as a home girl, the girl who loved coming home.

She travelled for work. Some jobs were like that. They required you to be mobile; they required you to be workhorses.

In the world at large, there were travellers who willingly left home, and refugees who fearfully lost home. There were whole land sites being taken over by rising water, by usurping oceans. In the Pacific, the Indian, land edges were rapidly disappearing, soft edges, were falling away as the oceanic waters lapped thirstily, siren-like in their desiring grasp, in their liquid tug and pull. Populated islands were going under. Amid war and drought, famine, fire and flood, whole nations were migrating.

Matilda. As a child, Tilda pondered her name, an eccentric sobriquet, a curiosity. In her country's context, Australia, Matilda meant swaggie, carrying one's sleeping arrangements, but, really, all of one's belongings, on the road. So Tilda flew off the beaten track, a misfired arrow.

She was bound for journeying, wandering off, losing her way, and having to find it again. As an Anthropogenic being, she would have to face nomadism as an adaptation to change.

Susan McCreery

BEETLE HEIGHT

BEDROOM is the last stamp on your passport. Across your chest, down the length of your skin (and bone), the weight of feathers. You are pinned. Butterfly, bird, chrysalis. Must we all desire flight? New horizons? You can see all the way to the end of your bed and this is far enough. Close one eye and your nose is a mountain, the world at its summit. Take a bath, they say, a lengthy lavender soak in the claw-footed tub. Listen to your heart beat, beat, beat (yourself up). Get outside, they say. Breathe the air of the seasons. *Take the air*. Take it with you. You know, without getting up, where your shoes are. Your FeatherLite (stop your) carry-on. Were it not for border control you would travel far. All the way to the kitchen to look out the window at the lengthening grass. It is spring, time for (passport) renewal. If you manage to crawl, beetle height, nose to earth, is this not enough? Expedition highlight: ladybird. Travel light, taking only air.

Paul Hetherington

TEXTS

Her text message sounded as the flight to Tokyo skidded a little on the runway before starting to accelerate. They had spent two days discussing their unexpected meeting in her hotel room, and now she said, 'see you in some future world or time zone'. He considered texting her about the zones they'd already crossed—having met at primary school and reconnected in an astonishing way—but couldn't think of the right phrase. His phone rested in his hand as he hesitated, eventually turning to the novel he'd promised himself he'd complete. The main character was a thirty-something woman on the wings of an affair, writing to her lover about the distances between them. 'How do we travel back,' she asked, 'to those luscious and hazy beginnings?' He immediately typed her words into his phone and sent them to her, hearing the immediate ping of her reply. 'I read it last week,' she said. 'But at least your kisses were all your own.'

Gayelene Carbis

WHERE DREAMS ARE MADE OF*

These times now are hard and harsh. I wake each morning with the thought of groundlessness. That table, this desk, might not fit into some unknown future; some place I might have to take off to because I won't be able to live any longer here – I remember other times, I remember flourishing. I remember saying to someone – I feel this sense of expansion. How I wasn't dehydrated but thirsty and full; how there was this flowering. I travelled, I took off, I was in Athens, I was in Delphi, I met women from all over the world at an International Women Playwrights' Conference. Even here in the city, in Melbourne, for a whole week, a Workshop, librettists and composers all siting together at one long table, and I met a woman there that took me to Alice Springs for the opera we worked on; and then later, a scholarship flew me to Banff to write poetry. At mid-day today I put on the television and while the rest of the world was watching the Presidential debate, I watched *Manhattan*, which made me cry and long for all the places I've /haven't/been.

* After lyrics from the song 'New York' by Alicia Keys

Bahar Razaghi

RECONCILIATION

When I think of my last visit to Iran, of the small village of Saghez, where my parents were born, I think of mountains crowned with snow and packs of feral children and dogs.

By the time I arrived in Saghez dusk had swept over the town like snow, leaving only a few street lights and illuminated windows. Though it had been a decade since I'd last visited my grandfather's house, once I left the taxi my feet could trace the path in the same way I could sing along the notes to a song I'd once loved, long ago, but forgotten.

I made my way through side streets and alleyways, my hair hidden under a hijab. Much of Iran was inflexible and rigid, and its people were crushed under the expectation of conformity. For all my time there I never saw any sign that it allowed for things which were different but, even so, graffiti sprung out between derelict buildings and alleyways, like a flower growing between cracks in pavement. A defiance, a shout of: *I am here, I am here, I am here*.

And I realise that despite the distance between Iran and Australia, people remain the same.

Dominic Symes

I DON'T NORMALLY LEAVE REVIEWS FOR MY AIRBNB HOSTS, BUT SINCE THEY INSISTED

'the wifi exceeded expectations'

& now I'm stuck for anything else to say. I'm trying to write this review before checking out, sitting on a bamboo mat on a floor in Yogyakarta. I could have spent all night kissing the smog from your mouth & spitting it back into the brown river, but instead we lulled the rats to sleep with our whispered suspicions, utterly in awe of their roof-shattering romantic aggressions, infinitely better suited to the conditions. Maybe it was just karma biting us back for lying to our host when we told her it was our honey-moon, but we didn't want to be disturbed & were kinda hoping that we'd get a discount. Plus, we knew we'd be leaving soon & couldn't have anticipated she'd ask to see our wedding photos. So we stayed up, unsleeping, to watch each other sweat above the sheets in this tiny bedroom without a mosquito net or an air-conditioner, but I guess it's best not to mention that. 'The teak furniture was beautiful'

& it was

Scott-Patrick Mitchell

RESORT

I hear it's sunny in the lounge this time of year. We don slippers and dressing gowns, grab coffee on the way, bask in sofa's morning glow. For lunch, we dress in trackies and singlets, dine from the luminous mouth of a café in the kitchen: we eat leftovers from the fridge. You go to fetch the mail. When you return, you show me photos of all the flowers you have seen in our faraway front garden. We spend the afternoon holed up in the cute library at the back of the house: the shelves in our study bristle and bloom with books. We read to each other. At dinnertime, we make our way outside to a gazebo, switch on the fairy lights, drink wine. The sun sets to reveal a sky, infinite with pinpricks of places other than here. We return to our hotel room, the bed we call cinema, the bed we call gondola-on-canal-of-dreams. We check the news: lockdown has been extended. Another fortnight inside this house. We make plans for tomorrow. You promise me a picnic on the front lawn. Excited, I can hardly sleep, unsure if my restlessness is actually ennui.

Angela Costi

HE TEXTED: PARTY AT THE CREEK

among the urban parkland of lanky eucalypts, arterial creek
beds holding streams of tears, the stew of grass soil and bug,
there lies a black dining handbag on the park's one and only tree
stump. for three days and two nights the bag made the hard wood
its bed. the bag looks spent and tired but still intact despite its
evident malnourishment. its metallic-gold chain snakes towards
the earth. its clasp locks the story in the pockets with the dried
mascara and cracked lip gloss.

mothers who believe in tradition and modesty gift exquisite
handbags for dining to their daughters when they become a
certain age for dating. if a bag is liked it can become the all
knowing friend. sitting on your lap from one train stop to another
or in a taxi swerving through amber lights. a sturdy bag stays
put at your feet while you move your upper body to a siren song
played on digital piano. it will stay open for you to find the card
for the hot pot and bubble tea for you and your man who can't
find his wallet tonight. and it will try to hide your phone before
it gets smashed.

Anne Elvey

WALKING

Brayakoolong Country, Stratford, Victoria

Graze of earthen breath exposes tender viscera as I pace a quiet town. Accounts speak along each other's tracks. Above the Avon, I read of students working for waterway's repair. Rough bunions and hollows declare that these red gums, at the edge of streets, pre-date colonial print, surviving plough, axe, trudge and bite of brine. A sugared trail has nesting holes, river views and red-browed finches foraging. I pass a school, a Shakespeare pub, the statue of McMillan positioned at the meeting of three roads. Explorer. Pioneer. Inscribed in stone words mask knowl-edge of massacres. They are told in a nearby park on a board speaking welcome to Country. Reports of children and church lie open on my notebook, while I walk beside a stir of leaves. Over bent course of trust, bridges toppled are remade. A diesel slows. Timbers sound across my settlerdom. The breeze does not collude. I find my place in a text where unstitched stories are sutured to scar.

Mube Nalbant

BLUE MORPHO AT THE EDGE OF TAMBOPATA

We were sipping blue morpho cocktails of rum, lemon, curaçao and maracuya. It was just before the rain season at the edge of Tambopata.

You were content with an insta worthy shot of a dead butterfly, a vivid blue morpho, flicking brown and blue when alive, making it difficult to capture with your camera. I was travel weary. You were planning the next expedition. I was pleased to stay with the certainty of macaws and capybaras, you were teased by a possibility of a glimpse of an anaconda or a jaguar. You had seen the blue side of a big butterfly. I was beguiled by the brown underside of her wings, her cloak with false eyes, to hide from predators, mostly humans. I understood your misunderstandings. You couldn't see; her scales reflecting the sunshine were perfecting that illusion of an iridescent blue without a pigment. I was fluttering through an Amazonian metamorphosis like a majestic butterfly, perceived as blue as I reflected.

I now reflect on the reason, as solitary as a blue morpho outside the breeding season, that nothing was as blue nor as brown as we saw just before the rain.

Kathleen Bleakley

PUTTING THE SUN TO BED

after viewing andré kertész's photograph 'coucher de soleil',
hungary, 1917

waking in our bed – middle of night – large space, draw bedding
around me. our balcony door opens up to sky, glimpse of sea.
in the morning i'll visit: you'll be sitting up in bed, your smile will
greet me at the door
waking in a bed folded out from a big purple chair, reach across
take your hand. have you got your bedding sorted you ask, yes
let's have a sleepover. wearing our star pjs, you in my purple top
me in your blue pants
waking: would you like a cuddle you hold your arms out. we stay
together head on my shoulder. you sleep deeply now in your
little bed a row boat, almost still just ripples of movement yours
or mine. lake Illawarra & beyond the entrance to ocean through
your window
just days before, we watched the lake's pelicans waddle, glide,
paddle, fly. you said my greatest wish is for your happiness
now nurses & i gently wash you i anoint you with lavender balm
they leave. beloveds circle take your hands sun streams in family
leave us entwined head on your chest hearing only my heart
waking at dawn: custodian of your quiet heart

Julia Prendergast

RHODES

We arrive in Rhodes in delirious darknight, a hilltop road beside
the church, more like a wide footpath.
I have no more ideas, says the cab driver...

We shift to the floodlit shopfront of Yasou's Souvlaki, pull out our
phones. A motorbike approaches from the steepside—*Yasou*'s in
white cursive script along the black belly of the engine.
We're lost, I say. *From Australia.*
I show him a photo of the house, zooming in on the green gate.
I know it, he says.

Daniel straddles the back of the bike. As the bike-light fades I
wonder if Yasou will kill Daniel, send his brother to rape me. I
see it in fast-time, until the scene is broken by a patch of road
that appears to be moving—a guts-out cat, limbs paddling, eyes
like tinned lychees.
Jesus-fucking-Christ.

Shining my phone-light on the rocky embankment—loose lichen
shifting like drifting seaweed at low tide. I'm fuckeyed—longing
for the rockpool sea.
Did I imagine the writhing cat? Guts like maggoty brain matter.
Why do we fester in each other?

I loosen a boulder, carry it closer. *It's okay darlingheart*, I say. Strobe-lit, I drop the rock on the cat's head.

Melina Thompson

AT YOTSUYA STATION

Half the platform is under construction, and the other is full of commuters. It's unsettlingly quiet. No crying kids or adults yelling into phones. I tug up my shoulder bag – it's going to snap under the weight of my books, soon. I've been eying an ¥80,000 backpack in the Atré at Matsudo. It's a bit dear, but it's not like the money's mine. I start to the right, trying not to get jostled by the flow of people all heading somewhere. I glance between my phone and the ground in front of me, but I've lost signal. I should have gotten a roaming sim card, but even the trains have free Wi-Fi here. I climb the stairs and break into open air, cloying heat on my skin, thoughts on the fan tucked away in my pocket. It's only then that my phone lets me know, very helpfully; I've taken the wrong exit. I'm on the opposite side of the huge station. If I had any confidence, I would turn around and head back into the throng. But I haven't seen my mum in months, and I let the crowd carry me the wrong way.

Lynette Hinings-Marshall

A NEW SAFEGUARD

Hot sands burn my bare feet as I peer at pale silhouettes of bathers in the shallow waters far from shore. I walk into the water toward them until the four women, all in white, back away. 'Anyeo hasseo,' I say. They stop, then giggle and drop their gaze. When one responds, 'Anyeo hasseo' I move closer. Each girl is wearing a white, long-sleeve muslin shirt and long, white muslin pants that cling to her wet, petite body. Tiny hands are clad in white cotton gloves. Most surreal is that each holds a white umbrella over her head to protect beautiful high cheekbones that whisper a Mongol ancestry.

For the two years I lived in Seoul I benefited financially from this determination by Korean women to safeguard their beauty. Every Monday morning I would walk up to the third floor of a building on Myeong-Dong for a one-hour Ginseng facial. This cost the ridiculously low sum of fourteen dollars and included Rose Hibiscus tea in the cosy lobby afterward. Today the same treatment 40 kilometres away costs me one-hundred dollars. I would happily pay this, but current lockdown rules in Melbourne restrict travel to five kilometres from home.

Seetha Nambiar Dodd

THE TOURISTS

If time travel is possible, where are the tourists from the future?
Stephen Hawking

The tourists have arrived. They are wearing functional shoes, multi-pocket accessories and glazed expressions. The journey was long, the seats narrow, the food salty. But they are filled with purpose, eager to immerse themselves into critical corrective missions.

They are among us, and easy to spot. Look out for this telling trait: they are *flustered*, conspicuously more so than you or I. There is no guarantee, you see, of landing in this precise moment again. Allowed only limited time, they move quickly. They make phone calls and amends. They are doing, they are undoing, hoping each subtle change will exponentially increase their future happiness. With an invested interest in the tourists' safe return, their future selves cheer silently from the blurred lines between the realms of here/there, now/then.

Those of us stuck in the ubiquitous present moment must take heed. As we are constantly reminded, yet carelessly ignore: the time, *our* time, is now. Of course, we could take a chance, wait for our invitation to travel, but it may never come.

Beth Spencer

GHOST FORESTS

The car is a capsule containing a family, insulating it from the outside while propelling it forward into the wide world.

If we got to visit a Roadhouse — those dream homes where you can order anything off the menu — our feet barely hit the ground.

Mostly it was Tip Top sandwiches on the bonnet of the Holden. With a thermos, and Cottees cordial in plastic mugs.

Sometimes we'd stop at a Milk Bar. Eight banana milkshakes! The owner scuttling to gather enough metal tumblers.
Finished? Dad would ask and I'd pass mine over and he'd drain it in a gulp.

Hours of driving through endless bare paddocks.

Then swinging off the Western highway to the Sisters Rocks to check our names were still tucked down low on one of the tors. (Trust British Paints — Sure Can!)

Mum would speed to make up time while Dad napped in the back, with the rest of us squished over and two lucky ones up front.

The faint smell of sick. (There was always someone.)

Singing 'There are rats, rats, as big as alley cats in the store...'

Just bring yourselves, the aunts would say, but the boot was always packed with baggage.

Danielle Baldock

THE DOGS OF WAR PLAY FRISBEE IN AN EMPTY HOTEL POOL

The pool in Zadar is full of soldiers. Shouts echo off cracked blue tiles, shiver off dry cement. Heartbeats like war-drums, you imagine attack.

All Spring echoes of war have swirled amidst the laughter on your Contiki bus. You've skirted French battlefields. Walked Mathausen with ghosts. In Gallipoli the cavalcades of graves are punctuated with poppies.

By Yugoslavia, the tour's theme song blares out amongst crackling radio warnings and war-talk over breakfast. Split is sharply struck off your schedule by shattering bombs. In Dubrovnik, you press your face against ancient stones, listening for whispers of nations rising and falling. The tour goes on, less laughing now.

Below you, haystacks of rifles lean like bonfires amidst the sun-lounges.

Black uniforms run and leap. You see now they're laughing with Henk and Kevin and Wayne, a red frisbee whirling. A soldier looks up, grinning with your brother's round cheeks. You wave, inscribe his face into memory.

Home, finally, you'll watch Yugoslavia exploding on the nightly news. Search faded newspaper-photos and smoky TV flashes, fingers tight-crossed he won't be there.

But for now the Dogs of War play frisbee in an empty hotel pool, laughing wild against the dark.

Heather Mackenzie

THE BUS TRIP

'Oh no, the Retirement Village Club's arranged another bus trip,' Jean said to Barb.

'What's wrong with that? Lockdown's lifted. I'm looking forward to a trip to the Coast and going to Pammy's Pie Shop for lunch.'

'But Barb, don't you remember last year's fiasco when Arthur and Jenny snuck off to a motel for *you-know-what*?'

'What?'

'You know.'

'No, I don't know. I wouldn't be asking if I did, would I?'

'Well, a bit of the other.'

'The other what?'

'Yes.'

'Yes? Yes? I don't know what you mean.'

'Thex.'

'Text? They texted someone?'

'No, no, to have … you know … thex.'

'Have you suddenly developed a lisp?'

'No, I just don't want to say it.'

'Say what for heaven's sake? You haven't actually said a thing.'

'I'm telling you I won't travel with people indulging in coits.'

'Why not? I play quoits with my grandkids, it's a good game.'

'Relations then.'

'What's wrong with my relations? They're no worse than yours.'

'No, Jenny and Arthur's relations.'

'I don't know any of them.'
'No, having them.'
'If I don't know them, why would I have them over?'
'Oh, I give up.'
'Good, I think you need to get out more.'

Eugen M. Bacon

THE HUNT

SHE is drawn to accented illumination from a disco ball flashing multi-hues on a DJ misjudging his skill, bodies 'shaking-it' on the dance floor. She sheds her skin, travels down onto a walkway bathed in moonlight, streetlamps dazzling back her glow of eyes, her hair.

Drunks, yahoos and the misplaced shadow her dusk stroll. *Swish, sashay*—she butters their hunger melting toward her. Their yearning is a desert, a desolate calling at the edge of something.

She allows a stamp on her wrist from a bouncer, tolerates fishbowl cocktails that glow in the dark. She'll listen to conversations, overlook spilt booze, wafts of smoke on leather jackets, an air of cheap sex on the dance floor, graffiti on the toilet walls.

'Be deadly.' She says to a clean face with a hint of slur. She likes his eyes, moonstone. 'You're a screamer. Get me a drink.'

Her response is an art, a spectre that gobbles love chants, injects a venom that turns humanity into leaves, crisp and hissing in a whisper of scales that brings them back to the nightclub again, again.

But, too soon, she'll swoon to the skies abandoning h u m a n i t y.

Dettra Rose

CASPER'S GALLEON

Casper's mum, Marina, was tall and skinny as a mast. Shoulders wide, hips narrow. As she walked, she swayed like a majestic galleon on the waves. Pale hair billowing, canvas sails. Casper and his mum read pirate stories and made sailing ships from wood and string.

But he blushed when she collected him from school. Kids teased she should live in a harbour or port. He reddened with shame. At home, she told Casper he'd grow up different, too.

He packed a rucksack and bought a train ticket to the last stop. Tiny sparks lit silver tracks. At his destination, kids were roller-skating and doing stunts on bikes.

They asked, 'What cool thing can you do?'

Casper shrugged and retrieved a pirate ship from his bag.

They said, 'Does that sail?'

'Yes, she does.'

At the pond, Casper whooshed his ship into the water. It wobbled, then tipped over. Casper almost cried. Then, it straightened and glided like a galleon on high tides.

'That's so cool,' the kids said. 'Can you show us how to make one?'

When Casper got home, he cuddled into his mum's heartbeat.

Later, he opened her bedroom door and there it was. The open sea.

Liana Joy Christensen

BLUE ROSETTA

Pieter finds the brochure in his in-tray. *Package deals! Executive Stress Relief Guaranteed!* He feels outed as a walker, someone verging on meltdown. But he still has a grip, witness the fact that he's corporate-smart enough to take the hint.

He flicks through the glossy pictures and is drawn to the diving tours of "New Atlantis". The Netherlands once more beneath the water. He looks at the fine print. Sure enough, it's the most expensive option, POA. But hey, the Corp's paying, so why not be a new kind of tourist in the old country.

When the CEO welcomes him back from the week's break, she congratulates him on looking so refreshed. He knows she feels smug about her capacity to avert staff burnout. He promises to share the vids on the social-club-stream.

Back in his office, he ignores the accumulated emails and looks through the picture window into endless smog. On his expensive plasti-veneered desk lies a fragment of Delftware, souvenired against all regulations.

Similar shards of impossible blue are to be found here and there in other high-rise offices. Indecipherable missives from a drowned world.

Shady Cosgrove

COVID TRAVEL

I thought it was a social media post and I was writing a brief word of encouragement. I didn't know I was buying a ticket to Vegas. Didn't know there would be trapeze artists in the hotel foyer or I'd be dancing in tassels at the bar. That down the road, Elvis and Lady Gaga would share the stage.

I didn't know I'd be sitting in that plastic booth, transfixed by the endless buffet and its conveyor belt of desserts. Or that you'd blow our savings on the roulette wheel and we'd take turns begging for spare change with an empty soda cup from McDonald's.

I had no idea you'd steal the officer's gun and hold it to my temple, laughing.

Last October, when your first message pinged, I couldn't imagine it would trigger a series of events that would leave me stranded in Vegas for almost a year, and I'd have to strike out alone – on foot – into the desert.

Christine Howe

THE LOOKOUT

Years ago, we camped halfway up the mountain, on a wooden lookout that no longer exists. Remember? The five of us carted sleeping bags and torches through the bush, stumbling over roots and stones until we reached the platform, perched on the mountain's dark flank. If we'd jumped, or leaned too far over the railings, we would have landed in a scratch of half-dead lantana. Instead, we squashed together on the slats for warmth, a tangle of elbows, laughter, beanies, knees. As we slept, cargo ships slunk through the night, and the city sprouted new subdivisions, identikit houses: whole manicured suburbs emerging from the coal wash. When we woke, years later, in the spitting rain, the lookout was gone. We had each crumbled down the slope, half asleep: you landed in Germany, remember? And his alarm went off in the United States – what I would give for the dig of your elbow now, the warmth of his laughter in my ear, and the lookout, floating over the lantana like a sentinel, unravelling the ephemeral.

Hilary Hewitt

MINDFULNESS

Each morning I swim. The water is inky, coloured by the tiles, by darkening clouds. I float on my back. Corfu (how long ago? which boyfriend?) – that luminous Grecian light, dissolving into air; sea as sky, sky as sea. Bees circle beside the pool, tiny wings whirring. Such hard work to stay aloft. The empty monastery, silence vibrating like a million bees, *roka* and thyme growing wild on the mountainside, the sweet scent of ecstasy. These rocket flowers are yellow as a child's sun. I pruned the plants yesterday, leaving plenty of buds. Bees are threatened; how hard is it to share? My grandmother set a place for her cat at mealtimes. (I was young enough to know this was normal. She knew I was unhappy.) I turn on my stomach as the first drops fall. Ripples spread. The human heart is 73 per cent water. How can Google be so certain about everything? What am I certain about? The scent of wild herbs. The liturgy of bees. That the heart is elusive, slippery as water.

Sandra Renew

THE AMAZING SINKING CAR

We're in the underpass, at the top of the bank out of the wind, leaning back on cool cement. Watching the deep swirl of current around the pylons, twelve-year-old fingers pinching the butts of hand-rolled durries. Silent, comfortable.

A Holden Torana, baby-shit brown, blue trim, ugly as, comes down the embankment beside us, doors and boot swinging open, headlights on, so fast it leaves the ground on the cliff edge, launches out over the water. Angles head down, dives for the bottom. Teddy bear in the rear window swings and waves.

Air bubbles stream to the surface, some sounding like rushing wind, others hesitant, emerging in slow gulps and glottal burps. Headlights burn, then dim and disappear as the last glimpse of chrome bumper vanishes.

We sit, frozen in the moment, not reacting, cigarettes burning down to our skin, eyes on the river and the amazing, flying, vanishing car.

Then, above us on the road, a scuffle of boots on gravel, voices coming loud then soft in the wind:

Mate, do ya think anyone saw us?

Yeah, no, no, yeah. Don't think so.

Mate, do ya think the water will wash off our fingerprints?

Yeah, no, no, yeah. Mate. Dunno.

Rananda Rich

LAST PLACE

Bertie, in seventh place, wondered how his garden and IT servers at home were holding up against irritating bugs.

First-placed Adam, meanwhile, realised he loved Evelyn. 'This magnificent prize,' he announced to disappointed supporters, 'becomes a punishment if I win.'

Bryony, second, choked up when she was disqualified two weeks later. Tearfully, she said: 'I am delighted to be pregnant.'

The remaining five candidates completed the invasive medical round. Oncology doctors removed the malignant lump from Dylan's testicles, though this removed him from the running too.

Harry failed the psychological tests, causing a furore about mental wellness discrimination.

Three contestants remained, including Bertie.

The six-month endurance round took place on the surface of Hawaii's volcanos.

Jenny was eliminated one month in when she failed to properly seal her survival dome.

Two candidates emerged intact in mind, body, and capability from *the ordeal*, according to Jim, or *paradise*, according to Bertie. Jim's unfortunate comment sealed the winner.

'Where aptitude is the same, attitude makes the difference at altitude,' the press release read.

Bertie commented, 'As the first citizen chosen to live on Mars, I look forward to pest-free gardening and unlimited space for my IT servers.'

Sue Brown

MEMORIES

Toilets. Some of my favourite travel memories. And every traveller has a toilet story.

Swanky loos with smiling attendants, western style, squats, holes in the ground and everything in between. Clean toilets, disgusting toilets. Communal toilets, unisex toilets. Toilets with spectacular views. Toilets with views of men at the urinal. You name it, I've used it.

Running to beat the queue, breaking all speed records, because a tour bus just pulled in. Using the men's toilet (with or without a sentry standing guard) because the queue for the ladies was too long.

Paper you buy from an attendant. No paper, so whatever you've got in your bag (did you really need that map?) Or, best of all, a bum gun, drenching everything around you.

And how do you flush? With your hands, with your feet. Or motion activated, flushing automatically when you stand or open the door (that one was a worry, I thought I was leaving things behind).

My favourite toilets are found in Japan. You need a degree to use them, but wow, they are amazing. They have heated seats, bidet jets and even play music so you can have privacy while you tinkle. Ecstasy!

Jo Tuscano

THE HARDEST TREK I'VE EVER DONE

I trek two hundred metres to the coffee shop. Forgot my mask. Two hundred back. One flat white, I say, holding my phone over the machine. Battery's flat. Two hundred back with a charged phone. Back at home, my partner's talking about vodka. It's 8.30 am. He travels the length of the hallway with our screaming baby, making shushing noises, sleep-deprived. I trek into my son's room. Not a lot of online learning going on there, so we walk him into the kitchen, sit him at the bench. There, we can pretend he really is on that plane to Queensland as I throw him some colourful packet of something loaded with sugar. Just like the ones on the plane, I tell him. I travel into sulky teenager's room. Still in bed. I've trekked 12,000 steps, according to the Fitbit.

Work from home. Make lunch. Clean. Rinse and repeat. I travel to different parts of Sydney during the day. I zoom to the northern suburbs, the east, west and south. I zoom over to my boss in the CBD. At 5pm, I'm zoomed out. Later, I'll sit with my partner. Vodka and Instagram. Sunsets and surf in Queensland. Perhaps next year, I say.

.

Brenda Proudfoot

ONE HUNDRED AND EIGHTY

April Fool's Day, 1841. Two dozen Marys, a score of Elizabeths; several Margarets, Sarahs and Janes. They're part of a consignment of 180 disgraced women drawn from the far reaches of Britain and herded on board the *Rajah*, bound for Van Diemens Land.

Matron Kezia Hayter, of the Millbank Penitentiary, divvies up the Quakers' benevolent gift. Yards of cotton material, scissors, needles and thread designed to keep the women meek and occupied during their 105 day voyage.

Nearly three thousand pieces of cotton fabric are stitched together to form an enormous quilt, marked by the pricked fingers of convicts. Seven red and green chintz birds swoop on the delicate garland of flowers embroidered on the central panel. Dozens of squares and triangles form intricate patchwork borders. The precision of seamstresses; the faltering stitches of amateurs distracted by a sailor or the swell of the sea.

Who were these women? Betsy? Grace? Caroline? Their quilt is a mysterious remnant of convict history, a rare artefact in the National Gallery of Australia, its journey through the centuries unknown. This testament to the artistry and humanity of a silenced underclass speaks to us through a time warp of one hundred and eighty years.

Angela Lloyd-Jones

BUSH COURTESY

The road was long and stiff. Dust had settled into the veins of the bitumen, a darkly compacted stripe through the Australian bush. Vehicles were only visible for *one... two...* and then no more, just a drizzle of light and exhaust drifting down the open road.

I was the final beacon for the regional drunkards, before the RSL turfed them out into their Utes, car keys tangled and clumsy with double vision. My courtesy bus diligently sputtered on at 10pm, and Pete, a regular, clambered through the door as I docked in the carpark by 11. The stale redolence, of last night's booze as well as tonight's, mingled with his sobs. 'My Joe...' He wailed. 'My bird's got out.'

'Can't have flown far, hey?' I reassured. His red-rimmed gaze met mine for a strange moment, but Pete said nothing. I watched the road, my high beams segmenting the bleary dark, aglow, reflecting a vast coalescence of foliage and tar, and suddenly something else.

The bus skidded, an unnatural caterwaul in the quiet. *one... two...* impact. Next to the carcass of the vehicle, a large emu stood serenely on the open road, gleaming despite the absence of light.

Joe padded away.

Tony Barrett

A SPOKESMAN'S LAMENT

'Why cycling is good for weight loss, fitness, legs and mind,'
Cycling Weekly

Helmet. Gloves. Trouser clips. High-viz jacket. Sunglasses. Lights, back and front (flashing). Pump. Backpack. And I'm off, jubilantly, hurtling down the driveway in my flimsy armour. Down the frosty, car-lined street, the shimmering Derwent in view; through the blood and boned Rose Garden, sharp right for the bridge rather than underpass.
I plunge into the seething CBD, a cauldron of carbon monoxide. Grim pedestrians keep their heads down, cars jockey for position. I feel the heat of sweating engines, the hiss of brakes, the impatient growl, the rev, the green-light roar. By way of protection I sing to myself '1.5 metres mate, 1.5!' hoping it will calm me, but I gesticulate angrily when an SUV squeezes me into the gutter. Jay-walkers in telephonic oblivion, sudden holes in the road, car doors flung open carelessly, P-platers veering blithely across my path, a vindictive curse hurled from an open window; all play games with my furious heart.
But the wheels keep going round and round
I arrive at work, lungs and calves aching, a sweaty fugitive, and tuck into a stress-quelling *torta caprese* from my favourite *pasticceria*.

Stuart Barnes

TRAVEL ~~BAN~~

dear fellow traveller, travelling through the dark, travelling with guitar—gla(a)d news travels fast (good light travels far, travels through the traveller-heart)—so travels the clear-eyed moon across the sea [somewhere i have never travelled]. tainted love travels on a tightrope at illegal speeds into several remote parts of Champagne. born in heartland, true love travels on a gravel road with the Count of St. Germain. travelled prawn, it is better to take the artery less travelled, to travel buoyantly than to arrive. bright big handle, bright big bowl—these could be for the travelling soul. we two travelling together—traveller's palm, traveller's joy—music for moon travels. euphonic, ungloved [traveller, your footprints] have love, will travel. star traveller, guitar traveller—travel queer, travel *here*

note: 'travel ~~ban~~' is part original, part cento, part remix from (in order): Sea Wolf's 'Dear Fellow Traveller', William E. Stafford's 'Traveling through the Dark', Debra Marquart's 'Traveling with Guitar', Tinnitus Relief's 'The Good Light Travels Far', Information Travels Through (Meftah album), Vachel Lindsay's 'The Traveller-Heart', So Travels the Moon (artist), E. E. Cummings' '[somewhere i have never travelled,gladly beyond]', Debbie Leggo's 'Love Travels On A Tightrope', Love Travels At Illegal Speeds (Graham Coxon album), Travels Into Several Remote Parts of the Brain (Northern Lights album), Backroad Traveler Band's 'Born in the Heartland', Elvis Presley's 'True Love Travels on a Gravel Road', Sylvia Plath's 'You're', Theo Croker's 'This Could Be (For The Travelling Soul)', Hiromi Itō's 'Two Traveling Together', Moonbrew's 'Music For Moon Travels', Euphonic Traveller (artist), Antonio Machado's '[Traveller, your footprints]'

Emma Ashmere

STIGMATA

I lied and ticked yes on the hospital discharge form. Yes I had somebody to stay with me overnight.

The house was as I'd left it. Lights on. TV muttering to itself. Strawberries blue with fur. Mangoes black with ants. My favourite cheese, a crusted stain.

And the knife. I'd bought it for you from a high-end chef shop during your sushi phase.

You'd been on your phone again, scrolling for a martini recipe, scrolling away from my birthday, towards the end.

There it is, you said.

It was after six but still so hot the fridge was juddering.

You picked up the knife, weighed it in your hand, said Is this yours or mine?

Your phone went off. Your ex again. You were still in your work clothes, tight trousers you wore for important meetings, shoes she'd bought you in Florence, or was it Milan.

You marched towards the balcony, elbow out. Lowered your voice.

I was drinking wine, shucking oysters, glancing at the TV. A bomb had gone off somewhere, sirens, panic, breaking news.

I won't be long, you said before you slammed the door.

That's when the knife must have slipped.

Arna Radovich

THIS IS YOUR CAPTAIN

On arrival in Shanghai, they follow the nose-in guidance system, set the park brake, shut down the engines. When all the procedural chatter is done, he leans back in his seat, pulls off his headphones, takes a breath. It's been a long flight.

A minder, mummified in PPE from head to toe, meets them on the aerobridge, escorts the crew through a terminal jewelled with crystals of sanitiser and white formless figures. His bag vigorously treated to a cloud of chemical mist.

At the hotel, locked in his room, food arrives on a tray delivered by a ghost. The only sound when he opens the door is of feet scuffling away down the long hall. Dinner comes in two layers of plastic and whatever it is, it's hard to recognize. He glances through the window at a scene bleached of colour—a terminal meld of sky and concrete.

Gone are the days of meeting up at the bar. Lost is the lubrication that kept the grind of loneliness at bay. Instead, for 39 hours he stares at four walls, scrolls robotically through hundreds of channels in Mandarin. Bores himself into a Netflix stupor.

Alyson Miller

VOID THOUGHTS

Vesna Vulović holds the record for surviving the highest fall without a parachute, a flight attendant who made it 10,160 metres and landed in pine and snow, peanuts still balanced on the tiny plastic tray—no, that part is a joke. But what isn't is the Kentucky meat shower, March 3, 1876, which is as it sounds, though whether it was mutton or venison, a human infant or the cartilage of a horse, no one is entirely sure. Locals blamed the buzzards, a group disgorgement over the bluegrass state, home of moonshine, tobacco, and large hungry birds. I asked you once what would happen if I, too, fell from that bridge or this plane or tumbled over the ledge on the hike you made me take, through death-trap, wild dog-pocked mountains disguised as romance, as adventure, as delight. The French call it *l'appel du vide*, the impulse to hurl oneself into the void, the call of nothingness that echoes in the unknown spaces of the reckless brain. Seven miles or 42,000 feet or 13,000 metres does not seem so far, but I ask if you remember the dress, the vintage one, in which to bury what remains.

Biographies

EMMA ASHMERE's short story collection *Dreams They Forgot* follows her novel *The Floating Garden,* which was short-listed for the 2016 Small Press Network Book of the Year. Her writing has appeared in *Overland, Meanjin, Griffith Review,* Commonwealth Writers magazine *adda,* and *Queer as Fiction.* She lives on Bundjalung Country in northern NSW.

EUGEN M. BACON is African Australian—her work has won, been shortlisted, longlisted or commended in national and international awards, including the Foreword Book of the Year, Bridport Prize, Copyright Agency Prize, Horror Writers Association Diversity Grant, Australian Shadows, Ditmar and Nommo Awards. Bacon's creative work has appeared in *Award Winning Australian Writing, Fantasy, Fantasy & Science Fiction* (Bloomsbury) and *The Year's Best African Speculative Fiction* (Jembefola Press).

DANIELLE BALDOCK's atmospheric writings capture small and vivid moments of time. She has been published in a quintet of Spineless Wonders' anthologies, lives in Sydney and takes lots of photos. Her favourite colour is green.

STUART BARNES is the author of two poetry collections: *Like To The Lark* (Upswell Publishing, 2023); *Glasshouses* (UQP, 2016), which won the Arts Queensland Thomas Shapcott Prize and was shortlisted and commended for two other awards.

TONY BARRETT lives in Hobart, Tasmania and as far as its big-dipper hills will allow, he rides his bike regularly. It is both delightful and perilous!

KATHLEEN BLEAKLEY has published five collections of poetry. her latest is *letters - a pocket poet (*Ginninderra Press, 2020). Her prose poetry has been published in Spineless Wonders collections: *Scars, Shuffle, Time* and *Writing to the edge.* Katheen lives on the NSW south coast.

SUE BROWN is a person who's always loved words, loved writing. She loves letting her creative juices flow with short stories.

GAYELENE CARBIS has been shortlisted for/won various awards, in Australia and internationally, including *ABR* Elizabeth Jolley, *The Age/*Readings, *Meniscus*, Lord Mayor's, and Fish (Ireland) short story prizes.

LIANA JOY CHRISTENSEN is the author of *Deadly Beautiful* (Exisle Publishing, 2011). Her awards include the 2020 Thimble Prize for Microfiction (USA), the Spilt Ink Prize for Creative Non-fiction and a shortlisting in the Newcastle Poetry Prize.

SHADY COSGROVE is the author of *What the Ground Can't Hold* (Picador, 2013) and *She Played Elvis* (Allen and Unwin, 2009). Her short works have appeared in *Best Australian Stories, Overland, Antipodes, Southerly,* and Spineless Wonders publications.

MOYA COSTELLO has four books, work in many scholarly and creative journals and anthologies (including from Spineless Wonders), has read at many venues, judged writing competitions and received writing grants. Adjunct lecturer, Southern Cross University.

ANGELA COSTI is the author of five poetry collections, including *Honey & Salt* (Five Islands Press, shortlisted for the Mary Gilmore Prize, 2008) and *An Embroidery of Old Maps and New* (Spinifex, 2021). Since 1994, her poetry and other texts have been published nationally and internationally, with recent works in: *Westerly*, *Live Encounters*, *Rabbit*, *Kalliope X*, *Rochford Street Review* and *Australian Poetry Journal*.

PS COTTIER edits poetry for *The Canberra Times*, and collects disturbing garden gnomes. Later this year the collection *V8*, written by PS Cottier and Sandra Renew, will be published by Ginninderra Press.

SEETHA NAMBIAR DODD lives in Sydney (such a lovely place) where she writes to remember, and sometimes to forget. Mostly at night, by the shimmering light of her laptop.

ANNE ELVEY is a poet, editor and researcher, living on Boonwurrung Country in bayside Melbourne (Naarm). Her poetry publications include *Obligations of Voice* (2021), *On arrivals of breath* (2019), *White on White* (2018) and *Kin* (2014). Her most recently scholarly work is *Reading the Magnificat in Australia: Unsettling Engagements* (2020).

A Belgian-born poet, **DOMINIQUE HECQ** lives in Melbourne. Hecq writes across genres and sometimes across tongues. Her works include a novel, five collections of short stories and twelve books of poetry. *Smacked* (2022) is fresh off the press at Spineless Wonders. With Eugen M. Bacon, she also co-authored *Speculate* (Meerkat Press, 2021), a collection of microlit.

PAUL HETHERINGTON is head of International Poetry Studies at the University of Canberra. He has published 16 poetry collections, including Her *One Hundred and Seven Words* (Massachusetts, MadHat Press, 2021). He has won or been nominated for over 30 national and international awards and competitions, recently winning the 2021 Bruce Dawe National Poetry Prize. He co-authored *Prose Poetry: An Introduction* (Princeton UP) with Cassandra Atherton.

HILARY HEWITT is an inner Sydney based writer. Her microfiction has appeared in literary journals and publications, including the *Anthology of Australian Prose Poetry* (MUP, 2020) and Spineless Wonders' curated Microflix, performance and festival events.

LYNETTE HININGS-MARSHALL is a restless professional woman whose desire for personal growth used travel as a means of realisation and change. She has lived in ten countries, each for two or three years, before returning to Australia. She uses flash fiction to capture memories of places and events.

RICHARD HOLT's microfiction collection, *What You Might Find* (Spineless Wonders, 2018) was described by *The Australian*'s Ed Wright as 'a tonic for readers in search of new angles from which to spin the world around in their heads'. Richard creates text-based installations and performances in public spaces.

HELEN HOPCROFT is an artist, theatre producer and writer based in Maitland. She once spent a year dressed as Marie Antoinette. Helen is currently reinventing herself as a poet/vocalist for The Majishans.

CHRISTINE HOWE is a writer and academic who teaches at the University of Wollongong. Her first novel, *Song in the Dark*, was published by Penguin, and her poetry and other short works have appeared in journals such as the *Griffith Review*, *Cordite*, *Island*, *TEXT*, and in various Spineless Wonders anthologies.

HOLLY IGLESIAS is a poet, translator, and author of two poetry collections: *Angles of Approach* (White Pine Press, 2010) and *Souvenirs of a Shrunken World* (Kore Press, 2008). *Hands-on Saints*, a chapbook, and *Boxing Inside the Box: Women's Prose Poetry*, a critical work, were published by Quale Press. She has received fellowships from the North Carolina Arts Council, the Edward Albee Foundation, and the Massachusetts Cultural Council.

PETER JOHNSON is an American poet, and novelist. His poems and fiction have appeared in *The Iowa Review, Indiana Review, Quarterly West, North Dakota Quarterly, The Party Train: A Collection of North American Prose Poetry,* and *Beloit Fiction*

Journal. Johnson is the founder and editor of *The Prose Poem: An International Journal*, and the editor of *The Best of The Prose Poem: An International Journal* (White Pine Press, 2000).

PENELOPE LAYLAND is a poet and former journalist and speechwriter. Her most recent book is *Nigh* (Recent Work Press, 2020).

ANGELA LLOYD -JONES is an 18 year old writer from Sydney. She creates based on experiences she has had, or would like to have. Mostly the latter.

HEATHER MACKENZIE can't tell jokes to save herself but loves writing short stories with a bite of humour. Tickled (and somewhat startled) to have won the occasional short story writing competition. Writing, gardening, raiding the local library and red wine in beautiful subtropical south-east Queensland. What more could you want in retirement?

SUSAN MCCREERY has authored three collections: *This Person Is Not That Person* (short stories, Puncher & Wattmann), *Loopholes* (microfiction, Spineless Wonders) and *Waiting for the Southerly* (poetry, Ginninderra Press). Her novel, *Scorched Linen*, is out on submission and she is working on a novella.

ALYSON MILLER's work, which focuses on a literature of extremities, has appeared in both national and international publications including three books of prose poetry, *Dream Animals*, *Pika-Don* and *Strange Creatures* as well the monograph, *Haunted by Words: Scandalous Texts*, and an edited collection, *The Unfinished Atomic Bomb: Shadows and Reflections*.

SCOTT-PATRICK MITCHELL (SPM) is a non-binary poet who lives as a guest on Whadjuk Noongar Land. They won MPU's Martin Downey Urban Realist Poetry Award and The Wollongong Short Story Prize in 2019, was shortlisted for The International Googie Goer Prize for Speculative Prose and Red Room Poetry Fellowships. Their debut collection, *Clean*, is due out in 2022.

CATHERINE MOFFAT is an award-winning short fiction writer living on Darkinjung country on the NSW coast near Newcastle. She is currently attempting the long, lonely haul of writing a novel.

MUBE NALBANT is a Sydney-based aspiring writer with a background in science and engineering. She likes putting words on paper to understand where she is coming from in order to prepare for where she is going to.

JONATHAN PENTON founded UnlikelyStories.org in 1998. His own poetry chapbooks include *Last Chap* (Vergin' Press, 2004), *Blood and Salsa* and *Painting Rust* (Unlikely Books, 2006), Prosthetic Gods (New Sins Press, 2008), *Standards of Sadiddy* (Lit Fest Press, 2016), and *Backstories* (Argotist E-Books, 2017). He lives in New Orleans, where he is currently working on a book of ekphrasis and collaborating with Cassandra Atherton on a book of haibuns.

JULIA PRENDERGAST's short stories have been longlisted, shortlisted and published: *Lightship Anthology* International Short Story Competition (UK), *Ink Tears* International Short

Story Competition (UK) *Glimmer Train* International Short Story Competition (US), Séan Ó Faoláin International Short Story Competition (IE), *TEXT* (AU), Elizabeth Jolley Prize, Josephine Ulrick Prize (AU). She lectures in Writing and Literature at Swinburne University in (Naarm) Melbourne.

BRENDA PROUDFOOT is a Lake Macquarie based writer and teacher. Her stories and poetry have been published by Catchfire Press, The Newcastle Herald, Hunter Writers Centre, Spineless Wonders and Blue Nib Press.

ARNA RADOVICH is a Blue Mountains-based writer with a particular interest in hybrid and short-form writing. Her work has been published in anthologies, journals, magazines and online, most recently in *Poetry for the Planet*, *ZineWest*, *Verity La* and *Meniscus*.

BAHAR RAZAGHI is a Kurdish writer based in Sydney who enjoys economics and gardening.

SANDRA RENEW's poetry collections are *It's the sugar, Sugar* (Recent Work Press, 202), *Acting Like a Girl*, (Recent Work Press, 2019) and winner 2020 ACT Writing and Publishing Award: Poetry; and *The Orlando Files* (Ginninderra Press, 2018).

RANANDA RICH, also known as The Ink Rat, is a 10,000-step-a-day, lifelong vegetarian and writer. Despite understanding the merits of an author platform, her dog, Ghost, is the one with a bajillion social media followers.

DETTRA ROSE is an award-winning flash fiction author. She wrote her first flash in 2018, winning the inaugural Australian Writers' Centre Furious Fiction prize – and a love affair was born.

BETH SPENCER's books include *Vagabondage* and *How to Conceive of a Girl*. *The Age of Fibs* (winner of the CBdL Award) will be published in an expanded print version in April 2022. She lives on unceded Guringai & Darkinjung land on the NSW Central Coast. www.bethspencer.com / @bethspen

DOMINIC SYMES writes poetry, some of which has appeared in *Overland*, *Cordite*, *Rabbit*, *Australian Book Review*, *Australian Poetry Journal* and *Best of Australian Poems 2021*. He curates NO WAVE, a monthly poetry reading series on Kaurna Country (Adelaide), and his first book *I saw the best memes of my generation* will be published by Recent Works Press in late 2022.

MELINA THOMPSON (They/Them) is currently a university student studying creative writing. She hopes one day that her writing can reach people and have an effect, even if she is just making people laugh!

JO TUSCANO is the author of the novel *The River Child* (Odyssey Books 2021). Her new novel *Under Andromeda* will be published by Odyssey Books in 2022. She is a co-author of *Back on the Block* (ASP 2009). She is a content creator for imagineer.me

PAUL VENZO has published widely on representations of identity; particularly in the fields of child and young adult literature, poetry, translation and gender and sexuality. Paul has been a visiting scholar with the Fondazione Cini, Venice, and is an alumnus of the Peggy Guggenheim internship program.

Editor

CASSANDRA ATHERTON is an award-winning prose poet and international expert on prose poetry. She was a Visiting Scholar in English at Harvard University, a Visiting Fellow at Sophia University, Japan, and is currently Professor of Writing and Literature at Deakin University.

Cassandra co-authored *Prose Poetry: An Introduction* (Princeton UP, 2020)and co-edited the *Anthology of Australian Prose Poetry* (MUP, 2020) with Paul Hetherington, her most recent book of prose poetry is *Leftovers* (Gazebo, 2020).

Cassandra has judged many literary awards, including the Victorian Premier's Literary Awards: Prize for Poetry, The Lord Mayor's Prize for Poetry and the *Australian Book Review* Elizabeth Jolley short story competition.

She is a commissioning editor for *Westerly* magazine, series editor at Spineless Wonders and associate editor at MadHat Press (USA).

The joanne burns Award

Each year Spineless Wonders auspices an award for the best writing in the forms of prose poem and microfiction in honour of foremost Australian experimental poet, joanne burns. The award is open to people residing in Australia and to Australians living overseas. Finalists chosen by each year's judging panel are offered publication in our annual anthology alongside invited writers.

The inaugural *joanne burns Award* was held in 2011 and was judged by joanne burns who selected Charles D'Anastasi's 'Madame Bovary' as the winning entry and commended Erin Gough's 'William Shatner vows to save the Great Basin Pocket Mouse' and Clare McHugh's 'Briefly'. All three pieces, along with those of other finalists appear in *small wonder*, edited by Linda Godfrey and Julie Chevalier.

The *2012 joanne burns Award* was judged by Carol Jenkins who selected Mark O'Flynn's 'under the maw of luna park' as the winning entry and commended Richard Holt's 'bush burial', Trina Denner's 'playing outside', Stu Hatton's 'down south' and Paul Mitchell's 'The Old Man and the Pool'. The winner and finalists all appear in *Stoned Crows & other Australian Icons*, edited by Julie Chevalier and Linda Godfrey.

The *2013 joanne burns Award* was judged by Shady Cosgrove who selected Mark Smith's '10.42 to Sydenham' as the winning entry and Hilary Hewitt's 'happy' and Mark Robert's 'cities that are not Dublin' as runners-up. All three pieces, along with those of other finalists appear in *Writing to the Edge*, edited by Linda Godfrey and Ali Jane Smith.

In *2014, The joanne burns Award* was judged by Angela Meyer and Richard Holt who selected Susan McCreery's 'Hold Up' as the winning entry and Kirsten Tranter's 'Turing Test Study Guide' and Mark Smith's 'The Meteorologist's Daughter' as runners up. All three pieces, along with those of other finalists are published in *Flashing the Square*, edited by Linda Godfrey and Bronwyn Mehan.

The *2015 joanne burns Award* was judged by Kirsten Tranter who selected Nick Couldwell's 'Dancing' as the winning entry. Runners up were Tim Heffernan for 'Butterflies in Iraq' and Matthew Gabriel for 'jesussaves82'. All three pieces, along with those of other finalists and invited contributors are published in *Out of Place* edited by Kirsten Tranter and Linda Godfrey.

The *2016 joanne burns Microlit Award* was co-sponsored by the Newcastle Writers Festival. The national category was won by Tim Heffernan for 'Barunga Conversation' and the Newcastle category, judged by Karen Whitelaw and Joanna Atherfold Finn, was won by Dael Allison for 'Breakwall'. The winning entries and finalists from both categories as well as invited contributors are published in *Landmarks* edited by Cassandra Atherton.

The 2017 joanne burns Microlit Award was co-sponsored by the Newcastle Writers Festival and judged by Cassandra Atherton. The national category was won by Tess Pearson for 'Traces' and the Hunter category was won by Luke Evans for 'You Can't Go Back'. The winning entries and finalists from both categories as well as invited contributors are published in *Time* edited by Cassandra Atherton.

The 2018 joanne burns Microlit Award was co-sponsored by the Newcastle Writers Festival and judged by Cassandra Atherton. The national category was won by Brenda Saunders for 'Birding' and the Hunter category was won by Jan Dean for 'Fish Flops and Flaps'. The winning entries and finalists from both categories as well as invited contributors are published in *Shuffle* edited by Cassandra Atherton.

The 2019 joanne burns Microlit Award was co-sponsored by the Newcastle Writers Festival and judged by Cassandra Atherton. The national category was won by K A Rees for 'No White M & Ms' and the Hunter category was won by Shaynah Andrews for 'The Ocean Has Made Promises'. The winning entries and finalists from both categories as well as invited contributors are published in *Scars* edited by Cassandra Atherton.

The 2020 joanne burns Microlit Award was co-sponsored by the Newcastle Writers Festival and judged by Cassandra Atherton. The national category was won by Jane O'Sullivan for 'Portals' and the Hunter category was won by Deborah Van Heekeren for 'If on an anxious Wednesday a dreamer'.

Winning entries and finalists from both categories as well as invited contributors are published in *Pulped Fiction* edited by Cassandra Atherton.

The 2022 joanne burns Microlit Award was co-sponsored by the Newcastle Writers Festival and judged by Cassandra Atherton. The national category was won by Penelope Layland for 'Gone, Absconded, Escaped, Disappeared' and the Hunter category was won by Catherine Moffat for 'The Light Remembered'. Winning entries and finalists from both categories as well as invited contributors are published in *Travel* edited by Cassandra Atherton.

About joanne burns

joanne burns grew up in Sydney's eastern suburbs. She worked as an English teacher in New South Wales, and for a time in London. She has taught creative writing in tertiary institutions, schools and community organisations. Her first collection of poems, *Snatch*, was published in London in 1972. Since then she has published more than a dozen further books of poetry. Her poems have appeared in numerous Australian literary journals, poetry magazines and have been set for study on the Higher School Certificate syllabus. joanne has been particularly concerned with the blurring of the distinctions between poetry and prose in her work, and has written extensively in prose poem/ microfiction forms. She has also written monologues and short futurist fictions and 'farables' (fables/ parables). Her latest collection *Brush* was published by Giramondo Poets in 2014. In 2016, she was awarded the New South Wales Premiers' Kenneth Slessor Literary Award for Poetry. A new collection of her work 'apparently' will be published by Giramondo Poetry in 2019.

Find more microlit at
SPINELESS WONDERS
www.shortaustralianstories.com.au

Spineless Wonders publications are available in print, digital and audio format from participating bookshops and online. For further information, go to the Spineless Wonders website:

www.shortaustralianstories.com.au